FLY GUY & FLY GIRL

NIGHT FRIGHT

Tedd Arnold

Cartwheel Books

An Imprint of Scholastic Inc.

Specially for Taylor, Mackenzie, Elaine, Vivian, and Logan!

Library of Congress Cataloging-in-Publication Data available

ISBN 978-1-338-54921-8

10 9 8 7 6 5 4 3 2 1   20 21 22 23 24

Printed in Malaysia 108

First edition, September 2020

Book design by Brian LaRossa

A boy had a pet fly.
He named him Fly Guy.
Fly Guy could say
the boy's name —

A girl had a pet fly.
She named her Fly Girl.
Fly Girl could say
the girl's name —

CHAPTER 1

One day, Buzz said to
Fly Guy, "Hey, let's go to
the zoo."

ZZZZOO?

That same day, Liz said to Fly Girl, "Hey, let's go to the zoo."

Buzz and Fly Guy
and Liz and Fly Girl...

...bumped into each other!

"Oh, hi, Liz," said Buzz.

"Hi, Buzz," said Liz.
"What do you want to
see at the zoo?"

"I want to see spider monkeys," said Buzz.

"Naked mole rats!" said Liz. "Let's go see both!"

Fly Guy said, "Wuzz-up?"
That's fly talk for "What do
you want to do?"

Fly Girl said, "Wuzza wuzza."
That's fly talk for "Let's do
something together."

CHAPTER 2

Fly Guy and Fly Girl went looking for some lunch.

Fly Guy found something sticky.

Fly Girl found something slimy.

Fly Guy found something slippery.

Fly Girl found something stinky.

Fly Guy and Fly Girl found
something scary.

Together, they flew into a dark, dark cave. Fly Guy said, "Gulpz." That's fly talk for "I'm not scared."

In the dark, dark cave they
found dark, dark woods.

Fly Girl said, "Gulpzie!"
That's fly talk for "I'm not
scared either!"

In the dark, dark woods
they found ...

...A FLY-EATING OWL!

19

Fly Guy and Fly Girl looked
for somewhere to hide.

They found a dark, dark box and
hid deep inside it.

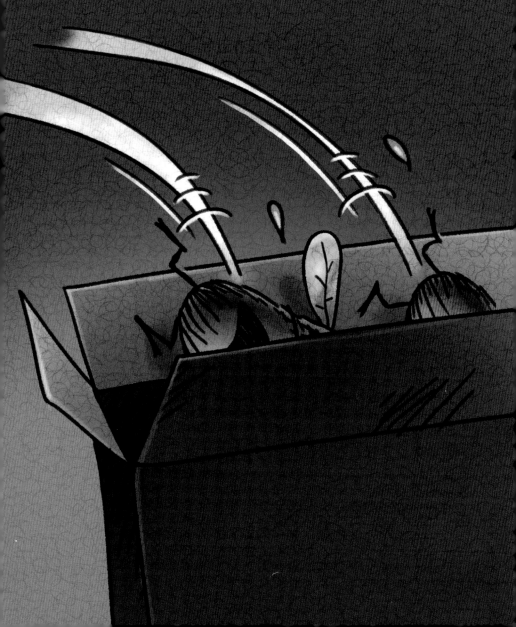

CHAPTER 3

"That was cool," said Buzz.

"I wonder where Fly Guy is."

CREATURES OF THE NIGHT

Liz said, "I haven't seen Fly Girl
either. Where could they be?"

"Where have you been?" said
Buzz. "We want to show you
two the cool night creatures."

Fly Guy and Fly Girl said,
"You must be kidding!
Absolutely not! Never again!
We're going home!" Which,
in fly talk, sounds like —